The Boxcar Children Mysteries

THE HOCKEY MYSTERY

created by
GERTRUDE CHANDLER WARNER

Illustrated by Hodges Soileau

ALBERT WHITMAN & Company
Morton Grove, Illinois

ISBN 0-8075-3343-2

1 3 5 7 9 10 8 6 4 2

Printed in the U.S.A.

Contents

CHAPTER 1

A Hockey Star in Greenfield

"He shoots — he scores!" Benny Alden shouted, racing down the ice. Although only six, he was a strong skater. When he reached the end of the rink, he threw his arms above his head and glided around in a circle, a victorious smile on his face. But a moment later he lost his balance and ended up sitting on the ice. "Ouch!" he said, getting slowly to his feet.

Benny's fourteen-year-old brother, Henry, skated up next to him.

"You okay?" he asked.

"Yeah," Benny said. "I guess I need to practice a little more."

It was open skating time at the Greenfield Rink, and the children were having a great time racing around the ice.

"I'll help you," Henry said, skating beside Benny. After the boys had circled the ice a few times, they decided to take a break. As they stepped off the ice, their twelve-year-old sister, Jessie, skated over. She'd been out in the center of the rink, practicing some turns. Their sister Violet, who was ten, joined them a moment later.

"Benny, I saw you zooming up the ice before," Jessie said. "Who were you pretending to be, Kevin Reynolds?" she asked, naming her little brother's favorite hockey star.

Benny's face broke into a big smile. "I wish! He's only the greatest hockey player ever!"

"I'm glad you think so," said a deep voice next to them. The children turned to see a broad-shouldered blond man standing beside them. When they realized who he was, their eyes grew wide.

"No way!" Benny said in amazement. "You're — you're — "

"Kevin Reynolds," the man said with a smile. He had friendly brown eyes and was wearing his Scouts jersey with the number fifteen on the back. Until he retired the year before, Kevin Reynolds had been one of the biggest stars in professional hockey. He had helped his team win the Stanley Cup five years in a row. He had been one of the leading goal scorers in the National Hockey League for ten years. And he had been chosen by the fans to play in the All-Star game twelve times.

"I don't believe it!" said Henry.

"And you are . . . ?" Mr. Reynolds prompted them.

"We're the Aldens," Jessie said. "I'm Jessie and this is Benny, Henry, and Violet."

Kevin Reynolds put out his hand and shook each child's hand firmly.

"What are you doing here, Mr. Reynolds?" Benny asked.

"Call me Kevin," he said, his eyes twinkling. "I'm doing the same thing you are — skating."

Benny looked confused. What was Kevin Reynolds doing at their little town rink? He was usually out on the ice with hockey greats like Wayne Gretzky — not regular people like the Aldens. "But why *here*?" Benny asked.

Mr. Reynolds laughed a deep hearty laugh. "I grew up in Greenfield," he explained. "I learned to skate right here in this rink when I was just about your age."

"That's right," Jessie recalled. "There are pictures of you and the whole Scouts team on the wall over there." She pointed.

"We were pretty sad when you retired last spring," Henry said.

"I've gotten too old to play professional hockey. Time to let some of the younger guys take over," Mr. Reynolds said. "You kids look like pretty good skaters. Are you going to play in the hockey mini-league?"

"What mini-league?" Benny wanted to know.

"I saw a poster about that in the lobby — it starts next week and goes for about a month, doesn't it?" Henry said.

"Yes," said Kevin Reynolds. "I'm coaching one of the teams — for twelve-year-old girls. My daughter, Catherine, is on it."

"Hey, I could play on that team," Jessie said.

"I thought you only liked figure skating," Benny said to Jessie.

"It's never too late to try something new," said Jessie.

"That's right!" said Mr. Reynolds. "Many of the kids in this league haven't played before. And I'm looking for an assistant coach. Henry, I saw how well you worked with Benny — how about helping out on my team?"

Henry's broad smile answered Kevin's question. "I'd love to," he said.

"Hey, what about me?" asked Benny.

Kevin looked at Benny thoughtfully. Then he squatted down so that his face was on Benny's level. He placed his hand on Benny's shoulder. "There's no team for your age group, but I'd be happy to give you some skating lessons after Jessie's practice is over."

Benny was so excited that he didn't know what to say. The other Aldens laughed, because they'd never seen him speechless before.

"That sounds great," Benny said at last.

"And you, too, Violet, if you'd like," Kevin added.

Violet smiled shyly and nodded.

"Great, then it's all settled," he said. "I'll see you here next week," Kevin called over his shoulder as he skated away. "Six A.M. sharp!"

"Six A.M.?" Jessie repeated. "It's still dark out then!"

"If you're going to play hockey, you have to get used to getting up early for practice," Kevin said. "That's when the rinks let us use the ice."

"Okay," said Jessie. "I guess I'll be getting up early!"

The Aldens couldn't wait to go home and

tell their grandfather they'd met Kevin Reynolds that day. They quickly packed up their things and headed back to their house.

After the death of their parents, the Aldens had run away and lived in an old boxcar they'd found. But as soon as they learned that they had a kind grandfather who was looking for them, they came to live with him in his big house in Greenfield. Their grandfather had even moved their old boxcar to the backyard so they could still play in it.

When they got home, Grandfather was sitting in the library in his favorite big leather armchair. He looked up from his book when the children came in. "How was skating?" he asked, putting the book aside.

"It was great!" said Jessie.

"You'll never guess who we saw at the rink!" cried Benny. But without giving Mr. Alden a chance to guess, Benny added, "Kevin Reynolds!"

"He's moving back to Greenfield," Violet explained.

"Yes, I remember reading something about that in the paper," Grandfather said. He picked up the *Greenfield News*, which was folded on the side table, and looked at the front page. "Here it is," he said, reading a headline aloud, " '*Hockey Star to Build New Ice Rink in Greenfield.*' "

"He's building a new rink?" Henry said. "He never mentioned that."

"It says here that they're still working on the plans, and then the town council has to approve them." Grandfather's eyes moved quickly down the article. "It also says Kevin Reynolds is coaching a team in the winter mini-league."

"I'm playing on his team," Jessie said.

"And I'm helping coach," Henry added.

"And he's giving Violet and me lessons!" said Benny.

"How exciting!" Mr. Alden said.

A week later, the Aldens got up very early to get ready for skating. Henry had helped Jessie pick out equipment and hockey skates at the pro shop at the rink. She put all of her hockey gear into her skating bag, which already held her figure skates and skating dresses.

"Can't you just wear your figure skates?" Benny asked when he saw Jessie putting her new hockey skates in the bag.

"No, hockey skates are different. They're harder and more padded to protect your feet. Also, the blades on hockey skates don't have teeth at the front, since you don't need to do any jumps or spins," Jessie explained.

Mrs. McGregor, their housekeeper, gave the children a hearty breakfast of eggs, toast with homemade raspberry jam, and orange juice. "You'll need lots of energy for skating," she said.

When the Aldens arrived at the rink, Henry went to find Kevin Reynolds and get ready for the team's first practice. Benny and Violet went up to the bleacher seats to watch. Jessie headed to the locker room to change, her stick in her hand and her large skating bag slung over her shoulder. She stopped at the water fountain, set her bag down, and rested her stick on top of it. Then she bent over to get a drink.

She had just finished getting the drink when she saw a small woman with a bouncy brown ponytail and a cheery smile coming down the hall. It was Tracey Lippert, her figure skating teacher for the past five years.

"Hello, Jessie!" Tracey called out. "Are you here to start working on a new routine?"

"Actually, I'm here to play hockey," Jessie said.

"*Hockey?*" Tracey repeated. "You're joking, right?" Then she noticed Jessie's bag with the hockey stick laid across the top and could see that it was not a joke. Suddenly Tracey's face clouded over. "You're playing on that mini-league team? The one Kevin Reynolds is coaching?"

Jessie nodded slowly, wondering why Tracey was upset. "Yes, I thought I'd give it a try."

"Then when are you going to have time for your figure skating?" Tracey asked

abruptly. "You could have won a medal in the All-County Championships this year."

"Do you really think I could have won a medal?" Jessie asked, her voice quavering. She'd never seen her teacher angry like this.

"Yes, you could have," Tracey said. "You're making a big mistake." And with that she walked off, her ponytail swinging behind her.

"Wow, she certainly was upset about something," said Violet, coming up behind Jessie.

Jessie stood stunned, looking after Tracey. "She doesn't want me to play hockey."

"Why not?" asked Violet.

"She says I won't have enough time for my figure skating," Jessie said. "But I don't know why she was so upset."

Violet looked thoughtfully after Tracey. "I don't know, either," she said. She took a sip of water from the fountain.

Jessie picked up her stick and hoisted her big bag over her shoulder.

"Want some help getting your equipment on?" Violet asked.

"Thanks." Jessie smiled. "That would be great." Together the two girls entered the locker room.

Jessie set her bag and stick down in front of an empty locker and began taking out her various pads and pieces of clothing. There were so many! She was used to wearing just a little dress and tights when she skated. But now she had to wear pads to protect her from being bumped by other players or hit by sticks or the puck. Over the pads, Jessie pulled on her practice jersey. She felt big and awkward. "I hope I'll be able to move in all this stuff!" she said with a laugh.

Henry was on the ice, talking to Mr. Reynolds. Benny stood by the glass, watching. Even though it was so early, several men and women were sitting in the bleacher seats to watch the practice. Some were there to see their daughters skate. Others wanted to see Kevin, the hockey star, up close. A few were members of the town council, there to learn more about the man who intended to build the new rink.

The Hockey Mystery

"Coach Reynolds is about to start practice," Benny called to Jessie.

Jessie made her way out to the end of the rink, where several girls had gathered around the coach.

A tall blond girl came up next to Jessie. "Hi, I'm Cathy Reynolds," she said.

"You're the coach's daughter, aren't you?" Jessie said with a friendly smile. "I'm Jessie Alden."

"Yeah, that's my dad," Cathy said.

"Welcome to Greenfield," said Jessie. "Where did you live before?"

"In New York City," Cathy said. "We just moved here last week. Maybe you could show me around."

"I'd love to," said Jessie. "Greenfield is a great town. After practice I'll take you to my favorite ice-cream place, The Scoop."

"Sounds good to me," said Cathy.

One by one, other girls emerged from the locker room with their hockey equipment. At last the whole team was assembled.

"In case you don't know me, I'm Coach Reynolds." His voice was loud and friendly. "The name of our team is the Polar Bears. My assistant, Henry Alden, is going to hand out jerseys and schedules at the end of the practice. We've got a great group of girls here, and we're going to have a great team — right?" He paused, and a couple of girls said, "Right, Coach."

"Come on, where's your spirit?" he asked. Then he repeated his question even louder. "Are we going to have a great team?"

"Yes!" the girls shouted excitedly.

Coach Reynolds laughed. "That's more like it! Before we start, why don't you each tell us your name and how much experience you have with skating and hockey."

Jessie listened as the girls spoke one by one. A petite girl with short black curly hair spoke first. "Hi, I'm Beth, and I don't have a lot of experience playing hockey, but it looks like fun!" She smiled at Jessie.

Some other girls had played on teams before. But many, like Jessie, hadn't even con-

sidered hockey until now. It seemed that
Kevin Reynolds's return to Greenfield had
gotten everyone excited about hockey.

Soon it was Cathy's turn. "I'm the coach's
daughter," she said. "I've been playing
hockey since I was little. I think I knew how
to hold a hockey stick before I could walk."

Everyone laughed. Since Jessie was standing next to Cathy, she was next. "I've been
skating for a long time, too. But I've only
done figure skating. This is my first time
trying hockey."

When she'd finished, Jessie turned to
Cathy and tried to catch her eye. But Cathy
looked troubled. Jessie wondered what was
bothering her. But before she could ask,
Coach Reynolds was starting the practice.

First he led them in some basic stretches
to loosen up their muscles. Then he had
them skate around the rink a few times, to
warm up and to see how well they skated.
Jessie felt good on the ice. She'd been skating since she was little and had gotten to be
very good at it.

Jessie noticed that the coach had sent

Henry off the ice to get something. She wondered what it was. As she made her last circle around the ice, she saw Henry come back empty-handed. He skated over to Coach Reynolds, and the two stood talking for a moment.

Now all the girls had finished loosening up and were ready for the next activity. But something was wrong. Henry and the coach were still talking off to one side. It looked as if something was bothering them.

"I know, but I put them there just last night," Jessie heard Kevin say. "I just don't understand," he continued. "Why would someone steal them?"

Henry said something quietly to Coach Reynolds.

Kevin thought for a moment, looking down the length of the ice. Then he turned back to Henry. "That's a good idea."

Henry skated quickly off the ice.

Benny was waiting by the glass. He'd heard what Coach Reynolds had said. "Henry, what's going on? Was something stolen?"

"I can't talk now," Henry said. "I'll explain later."

Henry was gone for just a few moments, but it seemed like forever. A few of Jessie's teammates began to fidget or adjust their laces. Kevin looked up toward the bleachers and shrugged. Jessie suddenly remembered that a group of parents and town council members were watching them practice. One man looked at his watch and frowned.

Finally Henry was back, his arms filled with mittens, gloves, and knitted hats.

"Great!" said Kevin when Henry had reached the center of the rink. "Spread them out the way we discussed."

"Okay!" Henry said. He then skated down the ice, dropping a hat or mitten every few feet.

"What do you think he's doing?" one of the girls said to Jessie.

Jessie shrugged. "I don't know, but I guess we'll find out soon."

Jessie glanced up at the small audience in the bleachers again. They were turning to one another with puzzled looks and pointing toward the rink. A few leaned in together and began whispering. A few others began shaking their heads. They didn't look happy.

The man who had been checking his watch stood up and shouted over to Kevin, "What does making a mess have to do with teaching kids hockey, Reynolds?" He pointed at the ice, which was littered with mittens and hats.

"You'll see," Kevin called back.

When Henry was finished, Kevin explained, "We're going to do some skating, stickhandling, and passing drills. I was planning to arrange some orange cones for you guys to skate around. You know, like you'd see on a highway where roadwork is being done. I bought them last night and put them in my office here. But when Henry went to look for them just now, they were gone! At first it looked like I might have to come up with a whole different set of drills! But Henry came to the rescue."

"You mean we're going to use the mittens and hats instead of cones?" Jessie asked.

"That's right," said Kevin. "He got a bunch of stuff out of the lost-and-found bin to use instead of cones." Kevin showed the girls how to skate around the gloves and hats, smoothly weaving in and out. Then the girls tried it.

Next, Kevin had them repeat the exercise with their sticks guiding the puck along the ice. At the end of the line, each skater had to pass the puck to the next skater. To make the drill more exciting, he divided the girls into two groups and set it up as a race. Jessie, Beth, and Cathy were on the same team. They lined up and watched as the other girls took their turns, cheering on their team to go faster.

The girl ahead of Jessie moved up the course, carefully controlling the puck with her stick.

When she had finished, she passed the puck to Jessie, who stopped it with her stick. Now it was Jessie's turn. She took a deep breath and set off. She had to concentrate hard not to lose the puck. She'd only recently started skating with a stick.

Controlling the puck, especially around things, was tricky.

"Go, Jessie!" she heard the girls on her team shouting.

Jessie was halfway done when she lost control of the puck. It slid off her stick and over to the boards.

"Oh, great," she heard someone grumbling. "That was a dumb mistake."

Suddenly Jessie realized it was Cathy talking. Why was she being so mean? Jessie felt her cheeks burning as she skated after the puck. She hooked her stick around it and got back to the course as quickly as she could.

"Come on!" Cathy called impatiently. "Hurry up!" She was next after Jessie and the last in their group to go.

Jessie managed to control the puck for the rest of the course and passed it to Cathy.

"Finally!" Cathy muttered under her breath as she started off. She zoomed up the course, weaving around the mittens and gloves easily. She never once lost control of the puck. But their side had already lost so much time that the other group won easily.

"Hooray!" the other group was cheering.

"Good job, everyone," Kevin said. As he went on to explain the next drill, Jessie stole a glance at Cathy. Cathy was looking straight ahead, her mouth set in a grim line. *This is supposed to be fun*, Jessie thought. *What's bothering her?*

CHAPTER 2

Strange Things Are Happening

When the practice was over, Henry handed out the light blue jerseys and gave everyone a printed schedule.

"Our first game is in a week," Kevin announced. "We've got to work hard to get ready. A regular season is usually fifteen or twenty games. But this is just a mini-league, to give you a little taste of what hockey is all about. So we'll have five games and then the final tournament at the end of the month. I'll see you all here the day after tomorrow at six."

After the team had skated off, Benny and Violet came onto the ice for their lesson with Kevin.

"Ready to work those legs?" Kevin asked. Violet nodded.

"We sure are," Benny said eagerly.

"I'll go put all these things back," Henry said, walking off with an armful of gloves, hats, and mittens.

"What do you think happened to the missing cones?" Jessie asked.

"Do you think they were *stolen*?" Benny asked, his eyes wide.

"Why would someone steal a bunch of orange cones?" asked Kevin. He smiled. "I'm sure they'll turn up sooner or later."

As Benny and Violet began their lesson, Jessie went to change out of her hockey gear. On the way to the locker room she passed her figure skating teacher, Tracey.

"What were you doing with all those hats and gloves on the ice?" she asked Jessie.

"We were doing a skating drill," Jessie explained. "Coach Reynolds was going to use cones, but they disappeared."

"They *disappeared*?" Tracey repeated.

"Coach said he put them in his office last night, and this morning they were gone," Jessie said.

Tracey rolled her eyes. "He's planning to build a whole new rink, and he can't even keep track of some cones?" And with that remark, she walked off.

Jessie walked slowly into the locker room. Beth had a locker next to Jessie's. "Hey, Jessie," Beth said. "Do you remember me? I'm Beth Davidson. I was in your figure skating class last year. With Tracey Lippert."

"Oh, yes! Hi," Jessie said.

"Tracey was pretty upset when I told her I wasn't going to be taking her class again," said Beth.

"She was upset with me, too," said Jessie.

"I love watching figure skating on TV," said another girl on the team. "Do you guys wear those fancy costumes?"

"Sometimes, for competitions," Jessie said. "But most of the time I just wear a regular skating dress with a sweater." Jessie dug in her bag and pulled out her turquoise dress. "Like this one. And these are my figure skates." She held them up. "I had to get different skates for hockey."

Jessie noticed that Cathy Reynolds was on the other side of the locker room. She had finished dressing and was watching her closely, but not saying anything. She had a strange look on her face that Jessie couldn't figure out. Then all of a sudden Cathy packed up all her gear, swung her bag over her shoulder, and began walking quickly out of the locker room.

The other girls were crowded around, chatting about hockey and figure skating and who their favorite teams and skaters were.

"Cathy!" Jessie called. "Cathy!" She'd been looking forward to showing Cathy around Greenfield. "Are we going to The Scoop?"

Cathy stopped walking and turned around. She looked very upset. "Not now. I've got to go. There's something I've got to take care of." And with that, Cathy was gone.

Jessie was left watching Cathy walk away. "First Tracey, now Cathy. What's going on today?" Jessie said to herself. She wondered what was so important that Cathy had to take care of.

Jessie sighed, then turned back to her locker and finished getting dressed. When she had packed up her things, she left the locker room with Beth Davidson.

A woman was waiting by the door. She was wearing a Scouts jersey with the number fifteen on it.

"Mom!" called Beth.

"Hi, honey! How was practice?" the woman responded.

"It was great!" said Beth. "Mom, this is my friend Jessie Alden. She's on the team, too."

"Nice to meet you, Jessie," said Mrs. Davidson.

"I like your jersey!" Jessie told Beth's mother.

"My mom has a jersey from almost every team," Beth said. "A couple of them are actual jerseys the players wore, with their signatures on them. Our house is like a hockey museum! We have pucks signed by famous players and pictures with their autographs, all kinds of hockey stuff."

"Sounds like you're a big fan," Jessie said.

"My husband and I love hockey," said Mrs. Davidson. "We have season tickets for the Scouts. So I couldn't believe it when I heard that Kevin Reynolds was moving back here!"

"Is that a real Kevin Reynolds jersey you're wearing?" Jessie wanted to know.

"No, it's just a copy. I'd do anything for a real one!" Mrs. Davidson said. "Or one of his signed sticks. Of course, they're much too expensive."

Jessie spotted Henry standing by the ice watching Benny and Violet as they finished their skating lesson with Kevin.

"Come meet my brothers and sister," Jessie said. She led Beth and her mother over to the ice.

"Thanks, Mr. Reynolds," Violet was saying as she stepped out of the rink.

"My pleasure," he replied.

Jessie introduced the Davidsons to Kevin and her sister and brothers.

"I'm a big fan of yours," Mrs. Davidson told Mr. Reynolds.

"Thank you," he said warmly. "Everyone in Greenfield has been so great to me."

Just then a thin, balding man walked over to join them. He moved gracefully, and the children noticed he was humming softly under his breath. "Hello, Kevin," he said in a quiet voice.

"Hello, Scott," Mr. Reynolds said, slapping him on the back. Kevin turned to the others. "Scott and I learned to skate together as kids. He runs this rink. And he's letting me rent space here while I get my own rink started." He turned back to his friend. "Do you know the Aldens and the Davidsons?"

"I'm Scott Kaplan. Nice to meet you," Scott said to the group gathered around Kevin.

"This is a great place," Benny said. "We love skating here. And the hot chocolate at the snack bar is the best."

"I'm glad you like it," Scott said, smiling. He turned to Kevin. "I was watching your practice. Why were all those hats and gloves on the ice?"

"Oh, that," Kevin said. "I bought some cones to use for that drill, but they disappeared. So Henry suggested using the stuff from the lost-and-found bin."

"I thought maybe it was some crazy Scouts drill," Scott teased his old friend, a big smile on his face. "I remember you were always a little unusual, but I didn't think you wanted the whole town to know that!"

"I was sitting with a man from the town council," said Mrs. Davidson. "He — both of us, really — wondered what you were doing with all that stuff on the ice."

"Better watch what you do, Kev," Scott warned in a joking voice. "The council may not approve the plan for your rink."

"Where is the new rink going to be?" Mrs. Davidson asked.

"On Overlook Road," Kevin said. "There's a big empty piece of land near the elementary school."

"That's what I'd heard," said Mrs. Davidson.

"We live right around the corner from there!" said Beth. "Cool! I'll be able to walk to the rink!"

Her mother did not look as happy. "I'm worried it will bring a lot of traffic and noise to our quiet little neighborhood."

"We've taken that into consideration," said Kevin. "We'll make sure it won't be a problem."

Mrs. Davidson did not look convinced. "Are the plans final?"

"Just about," Kevin said. "As a matter of fact, the architect just dropped off a set of plans this morning. They're in my office. Would you all like to come see them?"

"Sure," said Scott, speaking for everyone.

The Aldens exchanged looks. Mrs. Davidson sure looked unhappy about this new rink!

CHAPTER 3

An Unexpected Spill

After Benny, Violet, and Kevin got out of their skates, the group followed Kevin to his office, which was off the lobby. It was right next to Tracey's office. As they walked by, Jessie saw her old teacher inside, sitting at her desk filling out papers.

Kevin's office had a large desk in the center of the room and a Scouts poster on the wall. On his desk was a puck mounted in a glass box. Jessie picked it up and read the small plaque at the bottom: GAME-WINNING GOAL — STANLEY CUP FINALS. She also noticed a blue-and-red desk set with the Scouts logo on it and a bottle of ink and a fountain pen in it.

In the center of the desk was a large flat plastic envelope. Kevin picked it up and opened it. "These are the only set," he said, pulling out some large sheets of paper, "so we'll have to be careful with them. I couldn't wait to see them, so I asked the architect to bring them over right away — before they'd even made a copy."

"I'm sure they have this all stored on the computer, though," Scott assured Kevin.

"Normally they would, but they told me their computers went down last night," said Mr. Reynolds.

"Don't worry, we'll be careful," said Jessie.

Scott, Beth, Mrs. Davidson, and the Aldens all crowded around Kevin as he held the drawings up one at a time. The first showed what the outside of the building would look like.

"What a beautiful building," said Scott.

"Yes, I think it will be," Kevin responded.

He held up the next drawing, which showed how the rink and seats around it would look. There were some other drawings showing how the whole building would be laid out, with the lobby, offices, and locker rooms.

"Where's the snack bar going to be?" Benny asked.

Everyone laughed.

"Right here," said Kevin, pointing to a far corner on one of the plans. "And I'll make sure we serve hot chocolate."

"What will happen to this rink when the new one opens?" Violet asked Scott.

"I don't know," he answered. "But it won't be up to me. I'm retiring and moving out of Greenfield."

"Really?" Kevin said.

"Yeah. I've been thinking about moving for a long time — going someplace warm," Scott said. "I'll stay for the mini-league, but then I'm leaving."

Just then the phone rang. While Kevin spoke to the person on the other end, the others looked over the drawings.

"That was my wife," he said, hanging up the phone. "I'm going to go meet her for breakfast." He carefully replaced the plans in the large envelope and laid it on his desk.

"Now that you have the plans, what happens next?" Mrs. Davidson asked as she and the others made their way out of Kevin's office.

"The town council has to approve them," Kevin said. "I'm going to bring them to the meeting tonight. And assuming nothing unexpected happens, we'll start building at the end of the month."

Mrs. Davidson looked as if she were thinking about something. "Come on, Beth," she said, heading off. "Sounds great, Mr. Reynolds." She flashed a quick smile. "Assuming nothing *unexpected* happens."

Jessie and Henry watched as the Davidsons walked away. "What do you think she meant by that?" Jessie asked Henry.

"I don't know," Henry said. "It almost sounds as if she expects something to go wrong."

"I've got to run," said Kevin. He walked quickly to the main exit. "See you later!"

Saying a quick good-bye to the Aldens, Scott also left to go back to his office.

"I'm hungry!" Benny said.

"Didn't you eat breakfast?" Violet wanted to know.

"Yes, but it was so early I need another breakfast," Benny said.

"Let's get a snack after we skate some more," Jessie said.

"I noticed on the schedule that there's a special hockey practice session. We could work on your stickhandling, Jessie," Henry said.

"That's a great idea! Violet and I can skate more, too!" Benny called out.

Henry went to call home to let their grandfather know about the change in plans. They were happily surprised when, soon after, Mrs. McGregor arrived at the rink with a basket of warm muffins for them!

They skated for nearly an hour. Benny

and Violet skated around the outside of the rink, working on crossovers, which Kevin had taught them that morning. Henry and Jessie stayed in the middle, working on her stickhandling.

After a little while, Benny and Violet skated to the center. "Can we take a break?" Benny asked.

"Sure," said Jessie. "I'm ready for a break, too. How about a hot pretzel with mustard?"

"And some hot chocolate?" Benny asked.

"And some hot chocolate," Jessie assured him.

The Aldens walked out to the lobby. Suddenly they heard a shout from Kevin's office. The children looked at one another and then ran across the lobby. Tracey came out of her door at the same moment, and all of them went into Kevin's office.

"Coach Reynolds, what's wrong?" Henry asked.

Kevin was standing at his desk with his coat on, his back to them. He was looking down at his desk. He seemed to be frozen there.

"The plans for the new rink!" Kevin said. "They're ruined!"

Tracey and the children came closer and looked down at his desk. The plans they had looked at just a few hours earlier were spread all over the desktop. And something black was spilled across them.

"Quick, maybe we can save them," Jessie said. "Are there paper towels anywhere?"

"The snack bar will have some paper napkins," Tracey said. She ran out the door, with Jessie right behind her.

"What is that — ink?" Henry asked. He dipped a finger in the black liquid and looked at it more closely. Then he noticed the ink bottle lying on its side across the plans. There was only a little bit of ink left inside. "This must have spilled." He handed the nearly empty bottle to Kevin.

Jessie and Tracey returned with a stack of paper napkins. Everyone grabbed a few and tried to blot up the ink. But it was no use.

The ink had already soaked through the papers, destroying most of the drawings.

"How could this have happened?" Coach Reynolds asked. "I put the plans back in the envelope before I left. What were they doing spread all over my desk?"

"Do you think someone came in to look at them?" Jessie asked.

"And then they accidentally knocked over the ink?" Henry added.

"I guess it's possible, but wouldn't they have done something, instead of just leaving it here like this?" Coach Reynolds asked.

"Maybe they knocked it over as they were leaving and didn't realize," Jessie suggested.

"How could they not realize?" Kevin asked.

"Or maybe they were afraid to admit it — afraid they'd get in trouble," Benny offered. He remembered when he'd broken a glass bowl in the living room at home. He had been afraid to tell his grandfather. At last he had gotten up his courage and admitted what he had done. Grandfather had been proud of Benny for being honest.

"The plans are ruined now." Kevin sighed heavily. "I'd better call the architect." He gathered up the inky papers and shook his head. He looked very sad. "Now I won't be able to present these plans tonight. This will really set back the building of the rink."

Tracey and the Aldens left Kevin's office so that he could make his phone call. Tracey went back into her office. The Aldens looked at one another glumly. They all felt bad for Kevin.

"We might as well go get our snack," said Jessie. "There's nothing more we can do for Coach Reynolds."

When they were sitting at a table sipping hot chocolate, Benny said, "Do you really think someone spilled that ink by accident?"

"I don't know," said Henry. "It does seem pretty strange that someone would go in when Kevin wasn't there, take out the plans,

leave them all over the desk, accidentally knock over the ink, and then just
leave."

"What are you saying?" Jessie asked.
"That someone did it . . . on purpose?"

Henry nodded slowly.

"But why? Why would someone do something so terrible?" Jessie asked.

The children sat quietly for a moment,
picking at their pretzels. No one really felt
much like eating.

At last Henry spoke. "Maybe not everyone is happy that Kevin is building another
rink."

"You think someone wrecked the plans
because they were angry about the new
rink?" Jessie asked.

"Maybe," said Henry.

"Like who?" Jessie asked.

"Well, like Scott," said Henry. "If Kevin
builds that nice new rink, maybe no one
will come here anymore."

"But he's Kevin's old friend," said Violet.
"I can't believe he'd ruin the plans."

"And Scott's moving away anyway," said Jessie. "So it doesn't matter to him."

"That's right," said Henry. He took a bite of pretzel and chewed it slowly. "Well, what about Mrs. Davidson? Remember how upset she was when she learned that the rink was going to be right in her neighborhood?"

"I thought she was happy it would be so close," said Benny.

"No, that was Beth," Henry said. "Her mother was worried it would cause a lot of noise and traffic."

"But she's such a big fan of Coach Reynolds," Violet pointed out. "I don't think she'd do that."

"Can you think of anyone else?" Henry asked.

Jessie took a sip of her hot chocolate. Then she spoke. "I've noticed that Tracey seems really angry that people are switching from figure skating to hockey."

"Maybe she's worried that she'll lose her job if no one wants to take figure skating lessons anymore," Henry suggested.

"But do you think one of these people spilled ink all over the drawings?" Benny asked.

"They might have," said Henry. "Let's think about this for a minute. Which of these people knew that the plans were there?"

"Scott and Mrs. Davidson did," said Benny. "They were both looking at them with us."

"And Tracey's office is right next door, so she might have overheard us talking about them," Jessie said.

"Coach Reynolds said those were the only set of plans, remember?" Henry added. "So whoever did it knew that if they were ruined, it would cause a big problem."

"I just thought of someone else," said Jessie, eating the last bite of her pretzel.

"Who?" asked Henry.

"Cathy Reynolds," she said.

"Coach's own daughter?" Violet said.

"At first she seemed nice and asked me to show her around Greenfield," said Jessie. "Then all of a sudden she became really unfriendly — even a little bit mean during the practice. After practice, she said she had to take care of something and left in a big hurry."

Benny's eyes grew wide. "What did she have to take care of?"

"She didn't say," Jessie said. "But she would certainly know that her father had just gotten the plans. And she probably knew that he was going out to breakfast with her mom."

"That means she could have sneaked in and wrecked the plans," Benny said.

"What would her reason be?" asked Henry, crumpling up his empty hot chocolate cup.

"I'm not sure," Jessie said. "But it's hard to move to a new town and make new friends. Maybe she's angry at her dad for taking her away from her old school and her old friends."

Suddenly Benny sat up very straight in his chair. "I just thought of something else!"

"What?" said Henry and Jessie at the same time.

"Do you think that the person who ruined the plans also stole the orange cones?" Benny asked.

"Maybe," said Jessie.

Henry seemed doubtful. "I can see why ruining the plans would delay the rink's being built. But what would stealing the cones do?"

"Remember what Scott said?" Jessie asked. "The town council has to approve the rink. If they don't trust Coach, they might not let him go ahead with his plans."

"You mean someone might have stolen the cones to make Coach look irresponsible?" said Henry.

"Exactly," Jessie said. "In fact, that reminds me of something Tracey said when I told her about the missing cones. She said, 'He wants to build a whole new rink and he can't even keep track of some cones.' "

The Aldens gathered up their empty hot chocolate cups and crumpled napkins and threw them in the garbage. Then they put on their coats and got ready to leave.

"Is there anything we can do to help Coach Reynolds?" Benny wondered aloud.

"I think the best thing we can do," said Henry, "is keep our eyes and ears open and try to figure out what's going on — before anything else bad happens."

CHAPTER 4

A Secret Plan

A few days later, the Aldens were back at the rink for another practice. In the days after their talk in the snack bar, Jessie had gone to the rink for a few practices on her own. She was getting used to waking up early. She and the others had been watching for any other strange events. But no more mysterious things had happened.

"Do you think maybe we got carried away the other day, thinking that someone was trying to keep Coach Reynolds from building the rink?" asked Jessie.

"Maybe," said Henry.

"I still think there's a mystery going on," said Benny. "And I plan to solve it!"

Benny and Violet went up into the bleacher seats and sat down to watch the practice. Kevin had promised to give them another skating lesson when it was over.

Meanwhile, Henry laced up his skates and went onto the ice with Kevin. Jessie headed for the locker room to change. As soon as Jessie got onto the ice, she called out, "Hey, Coach!"

Kevin smiled at her. "How are you doing?"

"Fine," Jessie said. "Any news about the plans?"

"The architect is working on them," Kevin replied. "As soon as they're ready, I'll take them to the town council."

Jessie skated over to Cathy. "Hi!" she said. She wondered if Cathy would be nice today.

"Hello," Cathy replied with a friendly smile.

"Have you gotten to see much of Greenfield yet?" Jessie asked.

"A little bit," Cathy said.

Just then, Beth came onto the ice and waved. She skated over to Jessie in a figure skater's arabesque, her leg stretched out behind her. It looked funny in her hockey gear, and Jessie giggled.

"Do you miss figure skating?" Beth asked.

"I do," said Jessie. She turned back to Cathy. "So have you been to The Scoop yet?"

"The Scoop is the best," said Beth.

"No, I haven't been yet," Cathy said. Her voice was suddenly cool and she didn't seem interested in talking to Jessie.

"It's great — we could go today after practice," Jessie said. But as soon as she started talking, Cathy bent to fix her skate. Cathy acted as if she didn't hear Jessie.

Jessie was about to say something else when Coach Reynolds started the warm-ups. And for the rest of practice, there was no time to talk.

When practice was over, Beth and Jessie

were in the locker room, packing their gear into their hockey bags. "Want to come over to my house?" Beth asked.

"Sure!" said Jessie. "I'll tell my sister and brothers that I'll be home later."

A few moments later, the girls had slung their bags over their shoulders and were walking out to the parking lot. Mrs. Davidson was waiting there in a blue minivan.

"Hello, girls," Mrs. Davidson greeted them with a big smile.

"Hey, Mom!" Beth said.

"Hi, Mrs. Davidson," said Jessie, piling into the backseat with Beth. She remembered what she and her brothers and sister had talked about the other day. Now it seemed hard to believe Mrs. Davidson could be the one causing the trouble. She was so friendly and nice.

"How was practice?" Mrs. Davidson asked as she pulled out of the lot. Today she was wearing a New York Rangers jersey.

"Good," said Beth. "He worked us pretty hard."

"You're such a good skater," Jessie said.

"So are you," Beth responded.

"Not when I'm trying to control the puck," Jessie said.

"It just takes practice," Beth insisted. "You'll get it."

After they'd been driving for a little while, Beth pointed out the window. "See that empty lot?"

Jessie looked out and saw a large field surrounded by a few trees.

"That's where they're going to build the skating rink," Beth said.

They turned the corner. "And this is my street!" Beth said.

"Wow, you *will* live close to the new rink," said Jessie.

Mrs. Davidson pulled into the driveway of a yellow house and parked the car in the garage. "We're home!" she said.

When they went inside, Jessie was amazed to see that her friend had not exaggerated. The walls of the family room were covered with hockey posters. Draped over the couch was a blanket with the

Scouts logo on it. Several shelves on the bookcase held nothing but hockey memorabilia.

"Here's a picture of Mark Messier and Wayne Gretzky." Beth showed it to Jessie. "And here's a puck signed by Gordie Howe."

"Cool!" said Jessie.

"Let's get a snack," Beth said, leading the way into the kitchen. "I'm always really hungry after practice."

"Me, too," Jessie agreed.

Mrs. Davidson was in the kitchen, putting away some groceries and talking on the telephone.

Jessie hadn't been paying attention to Mrs. Davidson's telephone conversation, until she heard her say, "Yes, I've heard about the new rink."

Suddenly Jessie wanted to hear what Mrs. Davidson was going to say. But before Beth's mother said any more, Beth called out, "Mom, did you get more pretzels?"

Mrs. Davidson was listening to the person on the other end of the phone. "I know," she said. "The traffic will be horrible. I'm worried about it, too."

Again Beth said, "Mom, did you get more pretzels?"

"Just a minute," Mrs. Davidson whispered to Beth, her hand over the telephone receiver. Then she returned to the person on the telephone. "I know, I think — "

But her daughter interrupted her again. "Mom, we're hungry!"

"All right," Mrs. Davidson said to Beth. She turned her attention back to the phone. "Listen, I've got two hungry girls here just back from hockey practice, so let me call you later. But don't worry — I've got a plan. If it works, this rink definitely will not be a problem. Trust me." She hung up the phone.

Jessie couldn't believe what she'd just heard. What did Mrs. Davidson mean by "a plan"? Was it what Jessie and the other Aldens had been talking about?

"What can I get you girls?" Mrs. Davidson said.

"Mom, who was that? What were you saying about the rink?" Beth wanted to know.

"That was our neighbor, Mr. Rosen," Mrs. Davidson said. "Like me, he's worried about the rink causing noise and traffic here."

"So what are you going to do?" Beth asked.

Mrs. Davidson looked at the girls for a moment before answering. "Let's just say I have an idea about how to keep it from . . ." Mrs. Davidson paused as if looking for the right words. "From being a problem," she said at last. "You know what I always say: You can't just sit back and wait for things to happen — you've got to take action."

Why is Mrs. Davidson being so secretive? thought Jessie. Was it because her plan involved spilling ink and stealing cones?

"Now, about those pretzels . . ." Mrs. Davidson went to a cabinet to find the girls a snack.

Jessie took a pretzel from the bowl Mrs.

Davidson offered her. She tried to pay attention to the story Beth was telling her.
But she kept wondering just what Mrs.
Davidson's plan was. Why was it such a secret?

CHAPTER 5

Hidden Away

A few days later, Violet, Benny, and Grandfather were sitting in the stands for the first Polar Bears game. Jessie was in the locker room with the rest of the team, putting on her uniform. She was excited to be wearing her blue-and-white Polar Bears jersey. Henry was on the ice with the coach, getting ready for the game.

Benny and Violet looked around at all the people in the stands. There were parents, grandparents, sisters and brothers, and friends of the players. Benny spotted Mrs.

Davidson sitting with her husband. Violet noticed Scott Kaplan and Tracey Lippert sitting together.

"Hey, look, there's Jessie!" Benny shouted when he saw his sister skate onto the ice.

"She looks like a real hockey player in her uniform," said Violet, smiling proudly.

When all the Polar Bears were there, Henry led the girls in a quick skating and shooting drill to warm up. Then it was time for the game to begin. The other team was called the Cobras, and their jerseys were red.

Beth was playing center, with Cathy on her right wing and a girl named Joanne on her left. Each girl skated mostly in her own area of the ice, according to her position. As forwards, Beth, Cathy, and Joanne were supposed to lead the way up the ice, getting the puck away from the other team and shooting at the other team's goal.

Allison and Kaitlin were playing defense. They were taller than most of the other girls and very strong. Their job was to stay behind the forwards as the team moved up the ice. If the forwards lost control of the puck, the defense tried to get it away from the other team.

A girl named Susan was the goalie. She wore heavy pads over her legs and a mask to protect her face if someone shot the puck high into the net. Her gloves were different from the other girls', since she used them to block or catch the puck. Her stick was also different. It was flat and wide, because she used it to keep the puck from going in the goal.

As center, Beth began the game with the opening face-off against a tall girl from the Cobras. She and the Cobras' center stood in the middle of the ice. The referee dropped the puck and Beth got it. She drew it back to Allison, who quickly passed it to Cathy.

Cathy was a fast skater. She moved quickly up the ice. Beth and Joanne kept up with her. The three Polar Bears forwards passed the puck back and forth a few times as the Cobras tried to protect their goal.

Polar Bears fans in the seats yelled, "Shoot it!"

Coach Reynolds called out, "Good passing, girls. Now take a shot!"

At last Cathy saw an opening between two Cobras. She shot the puck, snapping her wrists hard, sending the puck toward the goal. It slid past the goalie's legs and into the net. The Polar Bears had scored! They were winning, one to nothing!

The Polar Bears fans roared from the stands. The extra Polar Bears players who had been sitting on the bench all stood up and cheered.

"Great shot!" said Beth.

"Good job!" Joanne added.

Cathy just gave a small smile.

The Polar Bears changed lines — a new group of girls came in to relieve the tired players. Skating up and down the ice was tiring. Unlike other sports, hockey players replaced each other frequently, only playing for a couple of minutes at a time.

"Jessie, play left wing," Coach Reynolds called. Jessie got up off the bench and took a deep breath. She felt nervous but excited.

The referee dropped the puck. This time the Cobras got control of the puck and began skating toward the Polar Bears' goal. But a moment later, one of the Polar Bears stole the puck away and the players moved back the other way.

"Jessie!" a girl named Shannon shouted, passing the puck to her.

Jessie stretched out her stick to catch the puck, but it slid just out of her reach. Jessie skated fast to try to catch it, but one of the Cobras got there first. The play moved back in the other direction. Jessie was disappointed she had not been able to get Shannon's pass. She knew she'd have to try harder.

When Jessie saw Coach Reynolds wave to her, she skated over to the side and Joanne went onto the ice to replace her. Jessie was glad, because she was breathless from skating so hard.

Over the next few minutes, the Cobras scored two times, but Shannon scored to tie the game. Then Cathy scored again, breaking the tie. Once again, the Polar Bears were winning.

A moment later the whistle blew, and the first period was over. The Polar Bears grabbed their water bottles and gathered around Coach Reynolds. "You're doing a great job," he told them. Then he gave them some pointers to improve their game in the next period. "We're winning by one goal," he reminded them. All the girls smiled.

Beth called out, "Hooray for Cathy and Shannon."

Jessie noticed that while Shannon was grinning from ear to ear, Cathy was frowning again!

Coach went on, "Keep up the good playing. Let's try to get a couple more goals."

The whistle blew, and it was time to start the next period. The Cobras scored in this period, tying the game. The Polar Bears struggled to score another goal but failed. When the period ended, the score was tied.

In the third period, Jessie was determined to do better. She concentrated on controlling the puck and didn't miss any more passes from her teammates.

Joanne and a girl named Marisa each scored once, but the Cobras also scored two more goals, keeping the game tied.

Jessie wanted to help her team, but no matter how hard she tried, she couldn't seem to score.

Soon there was only one minute left to go.

"Jessie!" Beth called, passing the puck.

But Jessie missed the pass. One of the Cobras raced past her and scooped up the puck. Before Jessie knew what had happened, the Cobra player had zoomed by, carrying the puck. Suddenly the girl was in front of the Polar Bears' goal, shooting. *Wham!* Before anyone could stop it, the puck slid into the net.

The Cobras were winning. Jessie felt as if it were all her fault.

There were still thirty seconds left in the game. Jessie decided she had to do something.

Cathy faced a Cobra player in the center

of the rink. Cathy took the puck away! She skated up the ice with the puck. Jessie and Beth kept pace with her. When they got near the goal, Cathy tried to shoot, but there were two Cobra players in her way.

"Pass it to me!" Jessie called. "I'm open!"

Cathy looked at Jessie and quickly passed the puck.

Jessie pulled back her stick and fired the puck. The puck flew through the air toward the net. But to her dismay, it went wide of the goal. The puck missed the net completely.

The buzzer sounded and the game was over. Jessie had failed to score and tie up the game. The Cobras had won.

After shaking hands with the other team, Jessie and the other Polar Bears skated slowly off the ice. As they walked back to the locker room, no one spoke.

Jessie slowly got dressed and began to pack up her things. She was almost ready to go when Beth called her over. "Hey, Jessie, can you fasten the clasp on my necklace?" Jessie left her bag on the bench and went to help her. Beth's necklace was a silver skate on a chain, which Jessie had often admired. As she attached the clasp at the back of Beth's neck, Beth whispered, "Don't worry, Jess. You tried your best." She gave Jessie a warm smile.

Jessie gave her friend a weak smile in return. She wished she could have helped her team win. "If only I hadn't missed that pass!" Jessie said. "If only I had scored at the end!"

"You'll do better next time," Beth assured her. "Want to go get something to eat?"

"No, I think I'll just head home," Jessie said.

When Jessie went back to get her bag, Cathy was standing right by her locker. When she saw Jessie, Cathy's face suddenly flushed. She looked as if she were about to say something. But then she seemed to change her mind and turned away. Cathy quickly gathered some things into her bag and left the locker room. She didn't even say good-bye.

Jessie wondered if Cathy was angry with

her because she'd made the Polar Bears lose the game. *I'll just have to try harder,* she told herself. Then she began putting the rest of her gear in her bag.

While Jessie was getting dressed, the Aldens were waiting by the rink for her. Henry was helping Coach collect and put away the equipment.

"Can I help?" Benny asked.

Kevin smiled at Benny. "Why don't you take the pucks back to my office." He handed Benny a bucket.

Benny reached in the bucket and pulled out a hard rubber puck. "They're cold."

"They have to be," Kevin said. "Other-wise they don't slide well on the ice. If they're too warm, they stick. Before the game we ice them down."

"I'll come with you," Violet volunteered.

"Thanks," said Kevin. "You remember where my office is, don't you?"

"Sure," Violet called over her shoulder. She and Benny walked quickly to the lobby. Next to the main entrance to the building, there were two closed doors.

"Do you remember which door it is?" Violet asked. The doors looked exactly the same.

"I think it's this one," Benny said, pointing to the door on the right.

Violet knocked on the door.

"Come in," a voice inside called.

Violet pushed the door open and saw Tracey sitting in a chair, looking at a catalog of skating costumes.

"Oh, hi, Tracey," said Violet. "Sorry to bother you. I'm looking for Coach Reynolds's office."

"You're Jessie Alden's sister and brother, aren't you?" Tracey asked.

"Yes," said Violet. "We just watched Jessie's first hockey game."

Tracey sighed loudly and rolled her eyes. "It worries me that so many kids are playing hockey these days. It's such a dangerous sport. I'm afraid somebody's going to get hurt — maybe Jessie. And when you watch the professional games, there's so much fighting."

"I love watching hockey," said Benny. "I love the fast skating."

"Sometimes players get a little rough, but it's still a great sport," Violet added. "And Jessie's team doesn't play rough."

Tracey shook her head. "I'd do anything to steer people clear of that sport. Anyway, Coach Reynolds's office is next door."

"Thanks," said Violet.

"No problem," Tracey said, turning back to the catalog.

Violet was just stepping out the door when something caught her eye.

In the corner of Tracey's office, partly hidden behind a chair, was a large stack of orange cones.

CHAPTER 6

The Rink at Night

"Did you see that, Benny?" Violet whispered when they had stepped outside Tracey's office and shut the door.

"See what?" Benny asked.

"The orange cones! In Tracey's office!" Violet said. "Remember at Jessie's first team practice, the orange cones were missing?"

"Yes," Benny recalled. "You saw them in Tracey's office?"

"Yes, in the corner, behind a chair," Violet said.

"Wow — do you think she stole them

from Coach's office?" Benny asked. "It's right next door."

"I can't believe she would do that," said Violet. "Why would she want to?"

"You heard what she said," replied Benny. "She wants to steer people away from hockey. Maybe messing up the practices is part of her plan."

"Maybe so," Violet said. She looked at the door next to Tracey's office. "This must be Coach Reynolds's office."

She knocked on the left-hand door and waited a moment. There was no response, so she opened the door slowly. It was dark and quiet inside. Benny found a light switch and turned on the light. Then he put the bucket of pucks on the floor next to the desk.

"Wait until Coach Reynolds hears about those cones in Tracey's office," Benny said.

But when he and Violet got back to the rink, Coach Reynolds was nowhere to be seen. Grandfather and Henry were standing by themselves, talking quietly about the game.

"Hey, guess what we saw in Tracey's office," Benny said. "The orange cones!"

"What?" Henry asked.

"We went into Tracey's office with the pucks by mistake," Violet explained. "And we saw a stack of cones there."

"Really?" Henry asked.

"She must be the one who stole them!" Benny said excitedly.

"Now, slow down," Henry advised. "Let's not jump to conclusions."

"That's right," Violet said. "There's no proof she took them."

"It is pretty suspicious," Henry said. "But we'd better not say anything until we have some more information. We don't want to accuse her of stealing, in case there's a simple explanation."

Just then Jessie came out of the locker room, walking very slowly and looking sad.

The Aldens did their best to cheer up their sister.

"You were great out there," said Benny.

"Not great enough to help us win," said Jessie.

Grandfather put his arm around Jessie's shoulder. "You can't win every game."

"Coach was really proud of how everyone played," Henry said. "And you'll all do better next time."

"You're right," Jessie said, looking around at her family, her face brightening. "I'm sure I'll do better at our next game."

"Now, how about a trip to The Scoop?" Grandfather suggested.

"All right!" Benny shouted, taking off for the exit. The rest of the Aldens looked at one another and laughed.

After studying the menus at The Scoop, they all ordered their usual favorites, and by the time they left the ice-cream parlor, Jessie didn't feel sad anymore.

That night, Jessie unloaded her equipment and uniform from her bag. Her clothes had to be washed before her next practice. "Hey, wait a minute," she said as she took everything out of the oversized bag. "Where are my figure skates?" Even though she hadn't been using them, Jessie had left her figure skates and dresses in the bag, buried under all her hockey gear. But now the figure skates were missing.

"Violet! Henry! Benny!" she called out. "Have any of you seen my figure skates?" No one had seen them.

"Maybe you left them in the locker room when you were getting dressed," Violet suggested. She remembered how much work it had been helping Jessie get dressed for her first practice. There had been so many pads and pieces of equipment — it would be easy to misplace something.

"I'm going back to the rink to see," Jessie said.

"Now?" Henry asked. "The rink closes in half an hour."

"Then I'd better hurry," Jessie said. "I love those skates. I've got to see if I left them there."

When Grandfather heard about Jessie's missing skates, he was happy to give her a ride to the rink. "I'll wait in the lobby while you check the locker room," he said.

The building felt very different at night from their usual daytime visits. A janitor was mopping the floor of the lobby. Instead of the usual noisy crowd, Jessie saw only a couple of people gathering their skating equipment and leaving the building. Jessie ran through the double doors to the rink. The bleachers were empty, and no one was skating. The surface of the rink was smooth and shiny.

Jessie ran down the dimly lit hallway to the locker room. Her footsteps seemed loud. When she reached the heavy door to the locker room, she stopped and grabbed the handle. She was just about to open it when she had the feeling someone was behind her. She quickly turned around. All she saw behind her was the long, dark corridor.

Jessie pulled the door open and stepped into the locker room entryway. Walking around a short row of lockers, she entered the main room. Only some of the lights were on, so it was dark in the corners. There didn't seem to be anyone else there.

But then Jessie heard a sound.

"Hello?" she called out. "Anyone here?" Her voice echoed in the large room.

There was no answer.

She walked slowly across the room to the locker she'd used that day.

Out of the corner of her eye, she saw something move. She stopped and turned quickly to see what it was.

Jessie smiled to herself when she realized it was just the curtain blowing on the slightly open window.

Jessie realized she'd been holding her breath. She exhaled. "It must just be a sound from outside," she told herself. This empty, dark room was giving her the creeps.

Jessie opened the locker and peered inside. No skates. "Hmmm, where else could they be?" she said to herself. Her eyes scanned the rows of lockers and benches. She got down on her hands and knees to look under the bench.

Just then she heard a sound. Jessie stood up quickly. This time she knew she had not imagined it.

Someone was in the locker room with her!

CHAPTER 7

A Surprise in Jessie's Bag

Jessie heard the locker room door shut, and she heard footsteps in the entryway. She could see someone's shadow against the wall. Jessie waited to see who would come around the corner.

A moment later, Cathy came in. When she saw Jessie sitting there, she stopped suddenly. She looked even more surprised than Jessie was.

"What are you doing here so late?" Jessie asked.

"I — I — I'm, um . . ." Cathy started.

"You were skating?" Jessie asked. "I mean, no wonder you're so good, if you're here this late practicing." Jessie laughed.

But Cathy didn't respond. She seemed nervous. She wouldn't look Jessie in the eye.

"So why are you here?" Jessie asked again.

"Oh, I was just, um . . . well, why are *you* here?" Cathy asked in return.

"I'm looking for my skates — not my hockey skates, my figure skates," Jessie said. "I just noticed they were missing from my bag."

"Well, I haven't seen them," Cathy said. "I was just here, um, doing some stuff." She grabbed her bag from her locker and quickly zipped it. "I've got to go. 'Bye." With that, she took her coat and bag and walked out.

Jessie still hadn't found her figure skates, and she wondered what could have happened to them. But there was another question bothering her: What was Cathy up to so late at the rink?

* * *

The next day, after hockey practice, something happened that was even stranger.

Cathy came out onto the ice late, so Jessie didn't have a chance to ask her any more about the night before. Coach Reynolds worked them hard, giving them lots of hard skating, passing, and shooting drills. When the hour was over, Jessie was worn out. She went to the locker room and changed back into her regular clothes. Then she joined her family in the lobby, carrying her heavy skating bag over her shoulder.

"I'm hungry," said Benny.

"Don't tell me — you want some hot chocolate," said Violet.

"What a good idea!" Benny said.

The Aldens walked to the snack bar. After choosing a small table in the back, Jessie sat down to get some change out of her bag. "Now, where is my coin purse?" she said to herself, digging through all the things in her bag. "I always leave it right on top."

"Don't tell me your things are out of order today," Henry teased his sister. Jessie was the most organized member of the family. Out of all the Aldens, she was the one who always kept everything in the right place and kept track of anything important.

Jessie smiled, but suddenly her smile disappeared.

"What's wrong?" Violet asked, seeing the strange look on her sister's face.

"I don't know," said Jessie. She began pulling things out of her large sports bag.

"What is it?" Henry asked.

"I thought I just felt something . . ." Jessie said, still pulling things from her bag.

At the bottom of the bag she saw something shiny.

Jessie pulled out her hockey socks and her jersey. She found the purse near the bottom, too.

There was something else at the bottom of her bag that was still partly covered by her skating dress. It looked like a skate blade.

Jessie reached down into her bag and pulled out — her figure skates!

"Weren't you looking for those last night?" Violet said.

"And I thought you said you hadn't found them," Henry added.

"I didn't," said Jessie. "How did these get back in my bag? I took everything out of my bag yesterday. They definitely were not in there."

"It seems as if someone *sneaked* them into your bag," Violet said. "As if they didn't want you to know."

"And the only reason someone would do that is if they'd taken them in the first place," said Henry.

"But why would anyone want to steal an old used pair of skates?" asked Jessie.

"And then why return them the next day?" asked Benny.

"I bet this has something to do with the other weird things going on around here," Jessie said.

"I'm much better at thinking about weird things on a full stomach," Benny said. "Let's get some hot chocolate!"

During the next two weeks, the Polar Bears played three more hockey games and won all three. Jessie played well. She made a few assists, passes to the players who then scored the goals. She was glad to help her team any way she could. But she was disappointed she still hadn't scored any goals herself.

One day after practice, Henry stayed on the ice with Jessie to help her practice shooting. Coach Reynolds gave Benny and Violet another skating lesson.

"Good work," he told them when their lesson was done. "You two have improved a lot."

Seeing that Benny and Violet were done, Jessie and Henry skated over.

"It looks like you're improving, too," Coach told Jessie, patting her firmly on the shoulder. "You'll score a goal for us soon," he assured her. "Now I've got to go meet with the architect who is working on plans for the rink."

"How are things going?" asked Henry.

"The architect is almost finished redoing the plans," Coach said. "The town council is meeting this Friday night. I'm hoping the plans will be done in time for me to bring them to the meeting."

"And the championship game is Saturday," said Jessie. "We'll be playing in it if we beat the Tigers tomorrow night."

"That's right," said Coach. "And if the plans for my new rink are approved, we'll have a party here on Sunday to celebrate. I've been busy lately getting ready for that."

"Anything we can do to help out?" Violet asked.

"No," Kevin began. Then he said, "Well, actually, there is something. I'm getting together a bunch of hockey stuff to display at the new rink — old photos, trophies, that kind of thing. If you kids could help me organize it, that would be a big help. Are you any good at organizing?"

The Aldens all looked at Jessie.

"Did somebody say organize?" Henry asked. "My sister is a champion organizer!"

"Just what I need," said Kevin. "Maybe we could get together one night this week and work on it."

"You and your family can come to our

house," Jessie suggested. "We'll make you dinner, and then we'll go through all your things."

"That sounds great," said Kevin. He thought for a moment. "Tomorrow is the Tigers game, so how about the night after that?"

"That's great," said Violet. "We'll just check with our grandfather. But I'm sure he'll be happy to have you and your family over."

"Grandfather is almost as much of a hockey fan as we are!" Benny said.

Kevin smiled broadly. "What can I bring for dinner?"

"We'll take care of everything," Jessie assured him. "Just bring the hockey stuff!"

"I left a box of things with Scott because I was going to ask him to help me," said Kevin. "But he's so busy. I'll pick it up from him and bring it to your house."

"We can get the box from Scott's office," Henry offered. "Then you won't have to worry about it."

"It's pretty big," Kevin said. "You may need two of you to carry it."

"That's okay," said Henry. "We'll ask our grandfather to come pick us up."

"You kids are the greatest," said Kevin.

The next night, the Polar Bears beat the Tigers seven to five. Jessie still hadn't scored a goal, but she was happy that her team was going to be playing in the championship game that weekend.

The next day, the Aldens were on their way to Scott's office to pick up Kevin's box. "I can't wait to see what's in it!" Benny said.

Scott's office was on the other side of the lobby, opposite Tracey's and Kevin's. The door was open, so the children poked their heads in. The office was dark and quiet. No one was inside.

Scott's desk was under the window, and large posters of Olympic figure skaters covered the wall. On the floor in the corner was a large box labeled KEVIN REYNOLDS.

"That must be it," said Henry. He lifted the top of the box and looked in. He saw some framed photos and a trophy. "Yes, this is it."

"I'll just write Scott a note so he'll know we took it," said Jessie. She went to Scott's desk and looked for a pad of paper and a pen.

Scott's desk was covered with papers.

"Wow, look at this," said Benny, holding up a brochure. On the cover was a picture of a beach lined with palm trees. *Florida's Most Beautiful Homes* was printed at the top.

"Remember he said he was thinking of moving somewhere warm?" Violet said. "I guess he's going to Florida."

Benny flipped through the brochure, admiring the pictures of sailboats and tropical fish.

"Here's a pen," said Violet.

"Thanks," said Jessie. She'd found a blank slip of paper and wrote Scott a quick note. Then she and Henry each took one end of the large box and headed to the lobby to meet Grandfather.

After dropping the box off at home, the children went to the grocery store. Because it was a special dinner, the Aldens had asked

Mrs. McGregor if they could make the meal. The children were very good cooks, so she'd agreed.

Once they were home, they got right to work. Jessie seasoned the chicken and put it in the oven to bake. Next she rinsed the string beans and trimmed off the ends so they'd be ready to steam for dinner.

Henry peeled and sliced apples for the pie.

Benny washed the potatoes and put them in a pot of boiling water.

Violet was in charge of the biscuits.

"Can I help?" Benny asked when he was done with the potatoes.

"Sure," said Violet, letting Benny have a turn stirring the biscuit dough. Then Violet and Benny took turns rolling it out into a thin pancake on the board and cutting it into circles. When it was time for dinner, they'd bake the biscuits so they'd be fresh and warm.

Then the Aldens set the table for dinner. They used the pretty flowered plates and bright blue napkins.

"Blue like the Scouts!" said Benny. "Kevin will like that!"

"And blue like the Polar Bears," Jessie added.

In a short while the doorbell rang.

"I'll get it!" cried Benny, running to the front door and pulling it open.

As expected, Kevin stood on the step. Beside him was Cathy and a small woman with brown hair.

"Hello," said Kevin, reaching out his hand to Grandfather. "You must be James Alden."

"I am indeed," said Grandfather with a big smile. "And I certainly know who you are."

"This is my wife, Amy, and my daughter, Catherine," Kevin said.

When everyone had been introduced, the two families settled in the living room. Jessie chatted with Cathy, who seemed friendly but a bit nervous.

A short while later, everything was arranged on the table, steaming hot and smelling delicious. "Dinner's ready," Henry called into the living room.

"Great!" said Kevin in a loud voice. "I'm hungry!"

"And so am I!" said Benny in his smaller voice.

Everyone laughed as they headed into the dining room.

The meal was a great success.

"You kids cook even better than you skate," said Kevin.

"Now can we look through your box of stuff?" Benny asked eagerly.

"We sure can," said Kevin.

The Alden and Reynolds families both went back into the living room and gathered around the large box. Kevin lifted the lid and pulled out a piece of paper. "Here's a list of everything that's in here," he said, handing it to Jessie. "I'm going to have all of this stuff on display at the groundbreaking ceremony on Sunday. You kids can help me decide how it should be set up. We also need to make signs explaining what all the pieces are."

One by one, Kevin pulled items out of the box and held them up. "Here's a pic-

ture of the whole Scouts team the first year we won the Stanley Cup," he said. Jessie checked the picture off on the list as everyone crowded around to see all the players they recognized in the picture.

"Here's a trophy I received back in college," Kevin said, pulling out a large silver cup. Jessie checked that off on the list as well.

"Everyone seems so excited about the new rink you're building," Grandfather commented.

"Not everyone," Benny said.

"What do you mean?" Grandfather asked.

"A few mysterious things have happened at the rink," Jessie said, "and they have made us wonder if maybe someone doesn't want the new rink to be built."

"What mysterious things?" asked Amy.

"The ink spilled on the plans," said Henry.

"And the missing orange cones," added Violet.

"You think those things are connected?" Kevin asked.

"They might be," Henry said.

"And there have been some other things missing, too," Jessie said. She was about to tell them about her skates when, all of a sudden, Cathy stood up.

"Dad, I have a headache," she said. "Can we go home now?"

"Oh, yes," Kevin said, putting his arm around his daughter. "I'm sorry you don't feel well."

"I'm sure I'll feel better if I just go home and lie down for a bit," Cathy said.

Grandfather got the Reynolds' coats as everyone said good-bye.

"I'll leave this box here with you so you can go through the rest of the things," Kevin said.

"We'll be happy to," said Henry.

After Kevin and his family had left, the Aldens sat down to see what else was in the box.

"Look, here's a picture of Kevin on his

first hockey team, when he was about my age," Benny said.

"And here's his Most Valuable Player award," said Violet.

Soon they had looked at everything and were putting the items carefully back into the box. Jessie was double-checking the list Kevin had made of everything in the box, making sure she'd marked everything off.

"Wait a minute," she said all of a sudden. "There are two things missing." She looked at the list one more time. "It says here, 'An autographed Kevin Reynolds hockey jersey,' and 'An autographed hockey stick.' "

"Those would be worth a lot of money, wouldn't they?" Benny asked.

"Yes," said Jessie. "And they're missing."

CHAPTER 8

Jessie Makes a Discovery

"Show me what's missing," Henry said, taking the list from Jessie.

"A hockey jersey," said Jessie, pointing to one of the items on the list. "And a hockey stick."

Benny and Violet crowded around to look at the list, too.

"They definitely weren't in the box," said Violet. "We looked at everything, and there were no jerseys or hockey sticks."

"We'd better call Kevin and let him know," said Henry, going to the telephone.

A moment later he came back.

"What did he say?" Jessie asked.

"There was no answer," said Henry. "Maybe they're not home yet."

"We'll have to tell him tomorrow at the rink," Violet suggested.

"That's right, tomorrow's our last practice before the championship game," said Jessie. "I'd better get some sleep!"

The next day the Aldens headed to the rink, as usual, before the sun was even up. Cathy was already in the locker room when Jessie came in.

"How are you feeling?" Jessie asked.

"Fine," said Cathy. "Why do you ask?"

"I was just wondering whether your head felt better," Jessie said.

"My head?" said Cathy.

"Remember, you had a really bad headache last night?" Jessie said.

"Oh, that . . . that's right . . . yes, it's all better," Cathy said, gathering up her gear and leaving the locker room. She moved so quickly, it seemed she didn't want to talk to Jessie anymore.

Meanwhile, out on the ice, Henry was trying to tell Coach about the missing jersey and stick. "Kevin, I have something important to tell you," Henry said, skating out onto the ice.

Kevin was studying a clipboard of information about his players.

"What is it?" Kevin asked, looking up, a serious expression on his face.

"It's about that box of stuff last night," Henry said.

Kevin broke into a smile. "Pretty neat, huh? For me it's like walking down memory lane, looking at all that stuff. Do you think you can set up the display?" he asked.

"Sure," Henry said. "Violet's going to make signs. She's a great artist and has really nice handwriting."

"Great. And thanks for dinner," Kevin said. "It was really delicious."

"No problem," Henry said. "But what I wanted to tell you was — "

"Listen, we've got to get the girls ready for the big championship game, so I think we'll need to talk about this later," Kevin said, going back to his clipboard.

"Okay, no problem," Henry said.

For the next hour, Kevin worked the Polar Bears like they'd never worked before. He had them skate laps and laps around the rink to strengthen their legs and made them do several intricate skating and passing drills. They ended with a shooting drill and a short scrimmage.

"Okay, girls, let's break now," Kevin said at last. "Come on over to the bench. I'd like to talk to you.

"Now, I realize some of you had never played hockey before when you started." He looked around at all the girls, making eye contact with each one of them. "And you've done a great job. You've played hard, you've practiced hard, and now you're seeing the result of all that hard work — tomorrow you'll be in the mini-league championship game. And I bet you're going to win that game, too. But whether or not you do, you should all be very proud of yourselves and of how well you've played.

"The game tomorrow is at ten o'clock. So I want you all to get a good night's sleep, eat a good breakfast, and come here ready to play. Ready to win. Let's go, Polar Bears!"

The girls cheered along with Kevin and Henry. They were excited about their game tomorrow. Jessie was especially excited. She was going to try her best. She hoped it would be good enough to help the team win.

After Coach's pep talk, Henry tried to get a chance to speak to Kevin alone, to tell him about the jersey and stick. But several players and parents were always around him. Finally the two were alone, and Henry spoke up. "Coach, I started to tell you something before practice," he began.

"Oh, yes, what was it you were trying to say?" Kevin asked.

"When we were going through the box, we noticed — " Henry began.

"Dad," said a voice behind him.

Henry turned around, and there was Cathy, her face quite serious.

"Yes, hon? What is it?" Kevin asked, his face concerned.

"I need to talk to you," said Cathy. "It's really important."

"Sure," Kevin said. "Henry, I've got to talk to my daughter. Can whatever you were going to tell me wait a little?"

"Okay," Henry said. He was disappointed that he still hadn't had a chance to tell Coach about the missing items. But he couldn't help wondering what was so important that Cathy had to talk to her dad about. She looked so worried. Henry hoped everything was all right.

Back in the locker room, Jessie was getting dressed in her usual spot next to Beth.

"Are you excited about tomorrow?" Jessie asked, pulling on her sweater.

"I sure am!" said Beth with a big grin. "We are going to win that championship trophy!"

Jessie laughed at her friend's enthusiasm.

"I think I'm cut out for hockey more than figure skating," Beth said. "Hockey is much more fun!"

"Do you think so?" Jessie asked. "I enjoy playing hockey, but I still like figure skating. I love the spins and jumps, the music, the costumes."

Beth was almost finished getting dressed. As usual, she asked Jessie to fasten the clasp on her silver skate necklace.

Jessie was turning around to help Beth when she spotted something. Something that made her eyes open wide.

Beth's skating bag was on the floor beside the bench, overflowing with hockey gear. But what was on top of the gear made Jessie stop and stare.

"Is that what I think it is?" Jessie asked.

Beth saw Jessie's expression and said, "Please don't tell anyone you saw it."

And Jessie knew that she was right.

Sitting on top of Beth's hockey gear was an autographed Kevin Reynolds jersey. Just like the one that was missing from Kevin's box.

CHAPTER 9

A Surprise for Jessie

"Beth, where did you get that?" Jessie asked, looking at the large blue-and-red shirt lying on top of Beth's bag. It had a Scouts logo on the front, and across one shoulder was a signature, written in pen, which clearly said, *Kevin Reynolds*.

Beth bent over and quickly stuffed the jersey into her bag and zipped it up. *"Please* don't tell anyone," Beth said again. Then she picked up her bag and left the locker room before Jessie could say anything else.

Jessie was left staring after Beth. She finished getting dressed and hurried outside as quickly as she could. But Beth was nowhere to be seen.

"What is it?" Benny asked. He had been waiting outside for Jessie. "You look upset."

A moment later, Henry and Violet joined them.

"You'll never believe what just happened," Jessie said.

The Aldens went over to the bleacher seats and sat down.

"I was talking to Beth in the locker room," Jessie said. "And her bag was on the floor next to us. And guess what was in her bag."

"What?" Benny asked.

"Kevin's jersey — the one that's missing!" Jessie told them.

"Are you sure?" Violet asked.

"Yes — I saw his signature on the shoulder," said Jessie. She shook her head. "When she saw me looking at it, she grabbed it and told me not to tell anyone! Then she ran out of the locker room!"

"That doesn't sound good," said Violet.

"I wonder if she has the stick, too," Benny said.

"We'd better tell Coach," Henry pointed out.

The Aldens went to Kevin's office, but the door was shut and locked.

"Maybe Coach is in his office right now with Cathy," he said. "After practice, she said she had something important to tell him and they went somewhere to talk."

"What do you think she had to talk to him about?" Violet asked.

"I don't know," said Henry. "She didn't say. It looked like it was something pretty important, though."

"I'll try to call Coach later about the jersey," Jessie said.

"In the meantime, let's go home and organize Kevin's hockey stuff the way he wanted us to," said Henry.

Back at home, the Aldens arranged the hockey items. The things from Kevin's childhood would be first. The display would begin with a picture of Kevin at age three, standing on the ice in tiny little skates, holding a hockey stick. Next would come his first trophy, won at age seven. Later in the display would be other trophies and things he'd won as a professional hockey player.

Using the information on the list Kevin had given them, Violet made signs explaining each piece. She used colored markers and wrote neatly on note cards. KEVIN REYNOLDS SCORED HIS FIRST GOAL IN THE NATIONAL HOCKEY LEAGUE WITH THIS PUCK, read one card. TICKER TAPE PARADE FOR THE SCOUTS AFTER THEY WON THEIR FIRST STANLEY CUP, read another card. THE COVER OF *SPORTS ILLUSTRATED* FEATURING KEVIN REYNOLDS, read another.

That night Jessie tried calling Coach Reynolds, but his wife told her he was out. "He's at the town council meeting," she explained. "Tonight's the night they're looking at the plans for the rink."

"I hope everything goes well," Jessie said before she hung up. She told the others what Mrs. Reynolds had said.

"I guess we'll just have to tell him about the missing things tomorrow," said Benny.

"But tomorrow is the big game," Violet pointed out.

"We'll tell him after the game," Jessie decided. "Now I'm going to bed so I'll be well rested for tomorrow!"

The next morning, the Aldens arrived at the rink excited and ready. Henry went right over to help Coach Reynolds prepare, while Jessie went to the locker room to get dressed. Violet, Benny, and Grandfather went to find seats. Even though they had gotten there early, the stands were already filling up with fans for both the Polar Bears and their opponents, the Sharks.

When Henry saw Coach, he asked him right away about the town council meeting the night before.

"I don't know," Kevin said. "Some of the council members liked the idea of a new rink. But others were worried about the rink causing a lot of traffic on that side of town and other problems. They're going to let me know later today. But you know what was really funny," he added. "Beth's mom was there. I saw her going in to talk to them after I left."

"That's interesting," said Henry. He remembered Jessie had overheard Mrs. Davidson talking about the rink and her "secret plan." He hoped her plan wasn't to convince the council not to build it.

"Anyway, I'm not going to worry about that now," said Kevin. "We've got a game to play!"

A short while later, the Polar Bears and the Sharks were on the ice, warming up for the game.

"Beth!" Coach called out.

"Yes, Coach?" Beth answered.

"I just realized we don't have any extra sticks in case someone breaks one," Kevin said. "Can you go to Scott's office and get some?"

"Sure, no problem," said Beth, skating off the ice.

The other girls continued their warm-ups.

"Uh-oh," Rebecca said as she skated beside Jessie, eyeing the other team.

"What's wrong?" Jessie asked.

"They look pretty good," said Rebecca. Like the Polar Bears, the Sharks were taking turns shooting the puck into the goal. Nearly every shot was a good one.

"They're undefeated this year," added Kaitlin as she skated past.

"Until today," said Cathy, joining the group. "We're going to beat them." She had a big smile on her face and looked excited to play.

Cathy seemed happier than she had in a long time, Jessie noticed. She wondered if her good mood had something to do with her important talk with her father the day before.

"That's right," agreed Jessie, smiling at Cathy. "We are going to be the champs."

Jessie saw Beth hand a couple of sticks to Kevin before she returned to the ice. Then the whistle blew and warm-ups were over. The starting players got into their positions.

Beth was facing a girl nearly a head taller

than she was, and in just a moment the Sharks were racing up the ice in control of the puck.

Wham!

One of the Sharks took a slap shot into the goal and scored.

"All right!" cheered one of the Sharks. Their fans roared.

"I told you," Rebecca whispered to Jessie, who was sitting beside her on the bench. "This is going to be a long game."

The next few minutes were indeed some of the longest Jessie could remember in any hockey game. The Sharks kept control of the puck almost the whole time. They were soon winning four to nothing. The Polar Bears had never been so far behind.

When Jessie was out on the ice, she tried her hardest, but wasn't able to get a shot on goal.

Near the end of the period, Jessie was skating quickly up the ice with the puck. *This time I'm going to score*, she thought. But when she passed one of the Sharks, she suddenly felt her feet come out from under her.

Bam! The next thing she knew, she was sitting on the ice.

A whistle blew. The player she'd just passed had tripped her!

With the Shark player sitting in the penalty box, the Polar Bears now had one more player on the ice than their oppenent. And they were not going to waste this power play.

But again, the Sharks quickly hit the puck all the way to the other end of the rink. Cathy knew what to do. Using her strong, powerful legs, she zoomed right up the ice and around a couple of Sharks. As soon as she'd crossed the blue line into the Sharks' end of the rink, Cathy pulled her stick back and — *smash!* — fired the puck at the Sharks' goal.

The puck went in — Cathy had scored!

All of the Polar Bears who were on the ice crowded around Cathy, and the others cheered from the bench. The fans in the stands cheered, too.

This time Cathy was smiling broadly, proud of what she'd done. Again, Jessie

wondered why she seemed so different today.

The period ended a minute later, and the
Polar Bears skated back to the bench, disappointed to be so far behind but excited by
Cathy's goal. After they'd rested for a couple of minutes and had some water, Coach
Reynolds gathered the girls around him.
"Now, I know they're a good team. But
you've just proved that you can score on
them. You've got control of the game —
don't let go of it!"

"Come on, Polar Bears!" cried Cathy, and
her teammates cheered.

The Polar Bears quickly scored a goal,
and then added one more a few minutes
later. Jessie played well. Although she
didn't score, she did have two assists.

When the whistle blew at the end of the
second period, the score was tied at four.

Sitting in the stands, Violet said, "Can
you believe it? In the first period they were
losing four to nothing! And now they're
tied!"

The Polar Bears were determined to win,

but the Sharks weren't going to give up that easily. They scored a goal and the whole Sharks team went wild.

"Don't lose steam," Kevin called from the bench. "Don't let them take control of the game!"

The Polar Bears knew their coach was right: They weren't going to give up now.

Over the next few minutes, the play went back and forth. Sometimes the Sharks seemed to be doing better, other times the Polar Bears did.

There was only one minute left in the game when Rebecca scored off a pass from Jessie. The Polar Bears gathered around, roaring with delight. In the stands, their fans roared, too. The game was tied again.

Benny turned to Violet and Grandfather. "Did you see Jessie's pass? That was great!"

Now it looked as if the game might go into overtime. Since Jessie's line had just come onto the ice, Coach left them on for the last few seconds of the game. Jessie was skating up the ice when Shannon passed the puck to her. Jessie decided to take a shot.

As she swung her stick, she suddenly heard a loud cracking noise. And when she looked down, she saw that her stick had broken.

Jessie dropped the stick and quickly skated over to the bench. Henry handed her an extra stick. It felt a little bit funny, but Jessie figured it was because she was used to using her own stick. She adjusted her hands. She didn't have time to think about it. There were only a few seconds left, and Jessie saw her chance.

The Sharks weren't expecting her to come back so quickly. So when Shannon passed the puck to her again, Jessie was wide open.

Here goes, Jessie told herself. She pulled back the stick and shot the puck toward the net.

To her amazement, the shot went in! With only seconds left to go in the game, Jessie had scored her first goal! And it was the game-winner!

Jessie's teammates swarmed around her, hugging her until she fell over with everyone on top of her. On the bench, Coach

Reynolds, Henry, and the other Polar Bears were jumping up and down with excitement. Looking up into the stands, Jessie spotted Grandfather and Violet and Benny on their feet cheering.

The game ended a few seconds later, and the Polar Bears and Sharks formed two lines and shook hands.

When the handshaking was done, Jessie did a little spin on the ice. Beth, who was near her, smiled. "You may have scored the game-winner, but you're still a figure skater at heart."

Jessie smiled back at her friend — and realized that Beth was right.

Now that all of the excitement was over, Jessie took a moment to look down at the stick she was holding, the one she'd used to score her first goal. No wonder it had felt strange. The stick was much longer than the one she normally used and looked completely different.

Then she saw that something was written on the stick.

Turning the stick sideways, she held the stick up so she could read it. *Kevin Reynolds, Stanley Cup Game-Winner*, it said.

"Oh, my goodness," Jessie said aloud. "This is the missing stick!"

CHAPTER 10

The Winning Stick

Jessie skated quickly over to Henry, who was standing beside the bench congratulating the players. Violet and Benny were with him. Grandfather was still up in the stands chatting with some of the parents.

"Henry, Violet, Benny!" Jessie called out.

"Hey, Jessie! You finally got your goal!" Violet said.

"And it was a great one!" said Benny.

"There's something I've got to show you," said Jessie, her voice urgent.

Now the other Aldens realized Jessie didn't look as happy and excited as everyone else.

"What is it?" Violet asked.

Jessie led them off to one side. "Look at this stick." She pointed to the signature.

"That's the missing stick, isn't it?" said Benny.

"How did you end up with it?" asked Henry.

"*You're* the one who gave it to me!" Jessie said. "Remember, when my stick broke?"

"I just picked it out of the bin with the extra sticks," said Henry. "How could it have gotten in there?"

"Wait a minute," Jessie said. "Beth went to get the extra sticks before the game."

"How did she end up with this stick?" Henry asked.

"I don't know," said Jessie. "I'm afraid the same way she ended up with the missing jersey."

"I think we'd better show Coach," said Henry.

The children didn't want to interrupt the

celebration that was going on around Coach Reynolds. All around him, players and parents were talking, cheering, and patting him on the back.

The Aldens waited until most of the people had left, and then they went over. "Coach Reynolds, take a look at this stick," said Jessie, holding it up for him to see.

Kevin took the stick from Jessie and looked at it. "This is my stick." He looked confused. "Where did you get it?"

"When my stick broke, Henry grabbed another and handed it to me. This was it!" Jessie explained.

"I don't understand — how did it get mixed in with the extra sticks?" Coach Reynolds asked. "Wasn't it in that box of stuff I gave you?"

"I'd been trying to tell you," Henry said, "but you've been so busy I didn't get a chance. There were two things missing from the box. One was this stick. The other was a jersey."

"The jersey I know about," Kevin said.

"You do?" said Benny.

"Yes, I can explain that later," said Kevin. "But the stick . . ."

"Remember you sent Beth to get extra sticks, from Scott's office?" Jessie said.

"That's right," Kevin said. "I think we'd better talk to Beth and Scott and see if we can figure out what happened."

Just then, Beth came out of the locker room.

"Beth!" Kevin called.

"Yes?" Beth said, coming over.

"Where did you get this stick?" Kevin asked her.

Beth looked confused. "Is that one of the ones I picked up from Scott's office?" she asked. "They were in the closet in his office. There were a couple together, and then one by itself. I just grabbed them all."

"Okay, thanks," Kevin said.

"No problem," Beth said. "Is something wrong?"

"No," Kevin said. "Nothing for you to worry about. You played a good game!"

"Thanks," said Beth, turning to go.

Kevin turned back to the Aldens. "Let's

go talk to Scott and see if he knows how this stick got into his closet."

As Kevin and the children walked to Scott's office, they went past Tracey's.

"Great game!" she said, stepping out from behind her desk.

"Thanks," said Kevin.

Henry caught a glimpse of the orange cones in her office. He took a deep breath and decided to ask Tracey what they'd all been wondering. "Um, are those Kevin's orange cones?"

Kevin looked where Henry was pointing. "Oh, that's what I should have done," Kevin said. "Borrowed Tracey's cones."

"So those aren't yours?" Jessie asked.

"No, she has her own," said Kevin.

"I use them for beginning skaters," Tracey explained. "Why — did you think I'd taken Kevin's?"

"Well, we did kind of wonder," Violet said.

"Why would I do that?" Tracey asked.

"Because you don't like hockey," Benny said. "You said it's too dangerous."

Tracey blushed. "You know, after watching a few of your games, I may be changing my mind. It is a great game to watch."

Kevin and the Aldens went on to Scott's office. Henry and Jessie reached the doorway first. They heard him on the phone. "Yes, that's right. I want the whole seating area around the rink refinished. And the lobby, too. The place will be as good as new — better than new."

Kevin poked his head into the office. Scott waved and mouthed that he'd be off the phone soon.

Kevin motioned for the children to wait outside until Scott had finished his call and then started to walk away. They could hear Scott saying, "In a couple of months? Great — I can't wait to see it! I can't wait until everyone in Greenfield sees it!"

Suddenly Henry looked at Jessie, his eyes wide. "Do you think Scott could be — "

"The one who's been causing all the trouble?" Jessie said, finishing her brother's sentence.

Henry nodded and caught up with Kevin.

"Coach, before we talk to Scott, could we talk to you for a minute in your office?" Jessie said.

Kevin looked at the children for a moment, wondering what they needed to talk to him about. "Sure," he said.

As soon as they were all in Kevin's office, Henry shut the door behind them.

"Coach," Jessie began, "we've noticed some strange things going on ever since you came to Greenfield. We think someone's been trying to stop you from building the rink."

"You mean by doing things like ruining the architect's plans?" Kevin asked.

"Yes, and causing trouble for you so the town council would think you were disorganized — like stealing the orange cones and hockey stick," Jessie added.

Kevin nodded slowly.

"We think it may be Mr. Kaplan," said Violet.

"Scott?" Kevin said. "But why?"

"He's probably worried about the new

rink taking too much business away from this rink," Henry said.

"But he's not even going to be here," said Kevin. "He's moving to Florida."

"Maybe that's just what he wants us to think," Jessie said. "But did you hear what he said on the phone just now? He's planing on redoing the whole rink. He said it would take a few months."

"That doesn't sound like the kind of thing someone would do if they were moving away," said Henry.

Kevin shook his head slowly. "No, it doesn't."

Just then, Scott came into Kevin's office. "Congratulations! Great game!"

"Thanks," said Kevin. "Er, Scott . . . there's something I want to ask you. Are you moving to Florida?"

"Yes, I am," Scott said. "I'll be out of here in a few weeks."

"So you're not worried about my building a new rink?" Kevin went on.

"No — no," Scott said. He sounded tense.

"That will be someone else's problem after I'm gone." He laughed nervously.

"Then why are you planning on redoing the whole rink over the next few months?" Kevin asked.

Scott looked around at the Aldens. "So you heard what I was saying on the phone?"

"Yes," Kevin said, his voice serious. "You're the one who ruined the architect's plans, aren't you?"

Scott sank down in a chair, his head in his hands. After a moment he looked up and nodded slowly, his face pale and grim.

"And you took the cones, and the hockey stick, too?" Kevin went on.

"Yes," Scott said quietly.

"But why?" Kevin asked.

Scott sighed. "I love this place — it's my whole life. If you build that new rink, who's going to want to come to this old place anymore? I'll be forced to close."

"But if you weren't really planning on moving, how come we saw a brochure about Florida in your office?" asked Benny.

"I thought about moving, but I can't do

it." Scott took a deep breath. "I know what I did was wrong, but I just couldn't help it."

Just then Tracey appeared in the doorway. "I have an idea that may help both rinks."

"Tracey — " Scott said.

"Yes, I heard what you were talking about," Tracey said. "I'm shocked at what you did, Scott, but I understand how you feel. With all this interest in hockey, I've been worried that there wouldn't be as many people taking figure skating lessons. And if that happens, then I'll lose my job."

"I still want to take lessons with you," said Jessie. She smiled at Kevin. "Hockey was fun, but I miss figure skating."

"I've missed you, too," said Tracey.

"So what's your idea?" asked Jessie.

"Kevin can focus on hockey in his brand-new modern building, and we'll focus on figure skating in this beautiful old building," Tracey suggested.

Scott slowly began to smile. "You know, I like that idea."

"If they *let* me build a brand-new modern building," Kevin said. "I still haven't heard from the town council."

"Hello," cried a loud cheery voice from the hallway. Mrs. Davidson pushed her way into the crowded office. She was wearing a Scouts jersey.

"Hey, wait a minute," said Jessie. "Isn't that . . ." She motioned to the jersey.

"Yes," Mrs. Davidson said. "It's an autographed Kevin Reynolds jersey. Beth and my husband bought it for me as a surprise. Wasn't that nice?"

"So that's why Jessie saw it in Beth's bag," said Benny.

"And why Beth didn't want me to tell anyone," said Jessie.

"And that's why you weren't worried about it," Henry said to Kevin.

"That's right," Coach Reynolds said. "I sold it to them. But I have others we can display."

"I just came by to tell you," Mrs. Davidson said, "the town council has agreed to let you build the rink."

"They have?" Kevin asked excitedly.

"Yes, thanks to me," she added. "They were worried about the traffic on Overlook Road, so I came up with a plan to add another lane on the highway and put in a stoplight."

"So that's what your plan was," Jessie said.

"Hooray!" cried Henry. "Coach Reynolds can build his rink!"

"And the Polar Bears won!" added Kevin.

"And Jessie scored the winning goal!" Violet put in.

"Let's go celebrate!" said Benny. "Hot chocolate for everyone!"

The next day was the big party to celebrate the new rink. The Aldens got dressed in their best clothes and drove to the Greenfield Rink. Kevin and his family were already there, greeting the mayor, members of the town council, and other people from Greenfield who were interested in the new rink. Tracey and the other skating instructors and all the Polar Bears were there with their families.

The Polar Bears had worked together with the Aldens to set up a beautiful display of Kevin's hockey memorabilia in the party room at the rink. As soon as the celebration started, Scott was going to present the Polar Bears with a trophy and the mayor was going to make a speech.

But before the speech was made, Cathy pulled Jessie aside. Cathy's face looked serious. "There's something I have to tell you."

"What is it?" Jessie asked.

"I'm going to be taking figure skating lessons with you," she said.

"You are? That's great!" Jessie said. "So why do you look so worried?"

"Well, there's something else I have to tell you." Cathy took a deep breath. "I was the one who took your figure skates."

"It was you?" Jessie said.

"Yes. I've always wanted to try figure skating, but with a dad who's a hockey player — well, you don't really have much choice," Cathy explained. "That's why I wasn't very nice some of the time — I think I was just jealous of you and tired of hockey."

"I noticed that sometimes you really didn't seem to care whether the team won or lost," said Jessie.

"That's true," said Cathy. "Anyway, I saw your skates in your bag, and I wasn't really thinking. I just grabbed them so I could try them out, see what they felt like. I always intended to return them. I tried to return them that night I saw you in the locker room, but I couldn't do it until the next day, when you left your bag open."

"Is that what you were doing here so late that night?" Jessie asked.

"Yes," said Cathy. "It was so much fun to try them — but I didn't want anyone to know."

"You should have just told me," said Jessie. "I would have been happy to lend them to you."

"Yes, I should have," Cathy said. She looked down and poked at the floor with the toe of her sneaker. "Anyway, I finally got up the nerve and told my dad how I felt. And he said he'd love for me to take figure skating. So everything's okay now. I hope you can forgive me."

"Of course I can," said Jessie. She smiled at Cathy. "Now let's go back to the party, friend."

Together, Jessie and Cathy walked back to the party room, where people were gathering to look at the display the children had set up. Henry, Violet, and Benny joined the two girls.

"I'm so glad you and your dad moved to Greenfield," Benny said to Cathy, grinning.

"We all are," added Henry, and Violet nodded.

Cathy looked at each of the Aldens. "You know," she said, "I'm glad, too."

GERTRUDE CHANDLER WARNER discovered when she was teaching that many readers who like an exciting story could find no books that were both easy and fun to read. She decided to try to meet this need, and her first book, *The Boxcar Children*, quickly proved she had succeeded.

Miss Warner drew on her own experiences to write the mystery. As a child she spent hours watching trains go by on the tracks opposite her family home. She often dreamed about what it would be like to set up housekeeping in a caboose or freight car — the situation the Alden children find themselves in.

When Miss Warner received requests for more adventures involving Henry, Jessie, Violet, and Benny Alden, she began additional stories. In each, she chose a special setting and introduced unusual or eccentric characters who liked the unpredictable.

While the mystery element is central to each of Miss Warner's books, she never thought of them as strictly juvenile mysteries. She liked to stress the Aldens' independence and resourcefulness and their solid New England devotion to using up and making do. The Aldens go about most of their adventures with as little adult supervision as possible — something else that delights young readers.

Miss Warner lived in Putnam, Connecticut, until her death in 1979. During her lifetime, she received hundreds of letters from girls and boys telling her how much they liked her books.